MONKEY MO GOES TO SEA

DIANE GOODE

THE BLUE SKY PRESS
An [illegible] New York

FOR PETER

THE BLUE SKY PRESS

Library of Congress catalog card number: 2001035993

ISBN 0-439-26681-5

10 9 8 7 6 5 4 3 2 1 02 03 04 05 06

Printed in Singapore 46

First printing, April 2002

Designed by Kathleen Westray

One morning a letter came for Bertie and Mo.

It said:

★ ★

Dear Bertie and Mo,

Meet me for lunch

aboard the *Blue Star.*

Love, Grandfather

P.S. Tell Mo to

act like a gentleman.

★ ★

So they went straight to Pier 17 . . .

. . . and boarded the *Blue Star*.

There were so many gentlemen on the ship!

Mo was sure he could act
like one of them.

So they went up the grand staircase,

and out onto the deck,

where Mo decided . . .

and he did everything the gentleman did.

Mo felt like a real gentleman.

He even looked like a real gentleman.

When he met Grandfather at lunch, Mo shook his hand.
Just like a gentleman.

He helped a lady
into her chair

and tried to make polite conversation.
Just like a gentleman.

He helped pass the fruit

and danced with two ladies.
Just like a gentleman.

Mo thought he was a real gentleman now.

But something was not right.
Everyone was angry with Mo . . .

. . . especially Grandfather.

"Mo," Grandfather told him, "if you cannot act like a gentleman, please leave the room!"

So Mo went out on deck.

Then, suddenly, he saw his gentleman go overboard.

And without thinking twice,
Mo jumped overboard, too.

Monkey see, monkey do!

He rescued the lucky gentleman . . .

. . . who gulped, and said,

"What a gentleman this monkey is!
He has saved my life!"

And Grandfather was very proud.